We hope you enjoy this book.
Please return or renew it by the due date.
You can renew it at **www.norfolk.gov.uk/libraries**
or by using our free library app. Otherwise you can
phone **0344 800 8020** - please have your library
card and pin ready.
You can sign up for email reminders too.

NORFOLK COUNTY COUNCIL
LIBRARY AND INFORMATION SERVICE

NORFOLK ITEM

The Story of Flying

Lesley Sims

Illustrated by
Stephen Cartwright

Reading Consultant: Alison Kelly
Roehampton University

Contents

Chapter 1

Into the sky

Not so long ago, people were stuck on the ground. They could only watch as birds soared above them. But some men were determined to fly.

In 1487, an Italian inventor named Leonardo da Vinci drew plans for a flying machine. He was sure it would fly.

Ha, ha, Leo! It's your silliest idea yet!

But he couldn't build one that worked, so no one believed him.

Twenty years later, a man called John Damian decided to copy the birds.

"I shall fly from Scotland to France!" he declared.

Wearing a pair of wings made from real feathers, he climbed to the top of a tower.

5

But John Damian didn't reach France. He didn't even reach the next village. Instead, he dived headfirst into a dung heap.

A French inventor, Clement Ader, decided to copy bats. He built an enormous pair of bat wings and stuck them to a steam engine. But that didn't work either.

Some people attached wings to
their bikes.

But they could never pedal fast
enough to lift off.

Inventors realized they would need more than a few feathers or a bike to fly. They would need a specially built machine.

In the 1850s, scientist Sir George Cayley built the very thing.

It was a glider
that was pulled
down a slope.
When a gust
of wind caught
under it, the
glider rose into
the air.

Sir George's coachman sat in the
glider for its first flight.
He didn't want
a second trip.

I'm off!

The problem with Sir George's glider was that it needed wind to fly. When Felix du Temple built his, he added an engine.

It ran down a ramp to gather speed... and it flew! But not for long. The engine was too heavy and it soon crashed to the ground.

Yet still inventors refused to give up. One day, they were sure, someone would build a plane that worked.

Chapter 2

The first planes

Wilbur and Orville Wright were brothers who lived in America. They built bikes, but what they really wanted to build were planes.

12

Their first machine was a glider
like Sir George's. In a strong wind,
it could lift off the ground on
its own.

Orville and Wilbur flew... and
crashed... and flew... and crashed.
But all the time, they were
learning about flying.

Then they built planes with engines. These had spinning blades called propellers.

The blades will push the air back and that will pull the plane forward.

Finally, they had a plane they were sure would fly. They were so excited they tossed a coin to see who would fly first. Wilbur won.

He crashed!

It took two days to fix the plane. Then, on December 17, 1903, it was Orville's turn.

Gently, he climbed into the cockpit and started the engine. The plane took off... and it flew!

But taking off wasn't as easy as it sounds. The Wright brothers had to build a track and pulley system to help. Weights were fixed to a rope which was tied to the plane.

Mechanics started the engine, the weights dropped and the plane shot along the launching track. This helped build up speed to lift the plane into the air.

Soon, lots of people were building planes. Most designers used engines developed from cars.

In 1909, the world's first-ever airshow was held in a field near Rheims, in France.

Yes! I made it up here!

Look at all those planes still on the ground...

Although 38 planes took part in the show, only 23 managed to take off. There were all kinds of competitions to see who could fly the highest, longest or fastest.

Nice tail!

How did he ever think *that* would take off?

Henri Farman won the non-stop flying prize. He flew 180km (112 miles) in just over three hours, without stopping to refuel.

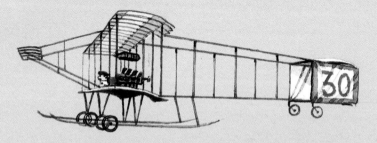

The prize for speed went to the *Curtiss Golden Flyer*, flown by Glenn Curtiss, which reached an incredible 75km (45 miles) an hour.

The largest plane at the airshow was the *Breguet I*. It was as heavy as a fully grown horse and as wide as a great white shark from wingtip to wingtip.

And they said it was too heavy to take off...

Many pilots had built their own planes using a wood or metal frame, which they covered in cloth. And most of them had stuck to the Wright brothers' tried and trusted design: the biplane.

But the star of the Rheims airshow was the pilot Louis Blériot. Only a month earlier, he had flown his single-winged monoplane across the English Channel and won £1,000.

He had set off from a field in France at dawn, excitedly climbing into the cockpit of his *Blériot XI*. It was the eleventh plane he'd built.

Half an hour later, he'd landed in Dover in time for breakfast.

For a while, the excitement of flying shook the world. But, by 1914, planes were no longer so new. Besides, with the First World War breaking out, people had other things on their minds.

Pilots began to fly spying trips across enemy land. Later, they even fought each other in mid-air... though some pilots didn't have much to attack with.

"We need planes built for fighting!" they cried, so plane builders stuck guns on the front. They went on to build bombers – planes with guns that could drop bombs too.

In Italy, plane designers built Capronis, which were enormous bombers. These had guns on the back as well as the front and carried enough fuel to fly all day.

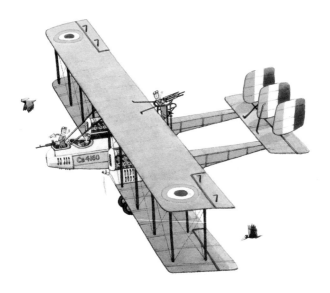

They also had flaps on the wings and three extra rudders on the tail, all to help the pilot steer as he soared over enemy land.

"Capronis are good," thought Anthony Fokker in Holland, "but I can build better!" And he produced a triplane, with three wings on each side. Not only could it turn more quickly, it was an incredibly fast flyer.

You'll never catch me!

"I want one!" cried the Red Baron, who was a terrifying German pilot. He went on to shoot down a record 80 enemy planes from his Fokker triplane.

Chapter 3

A lot of hot air

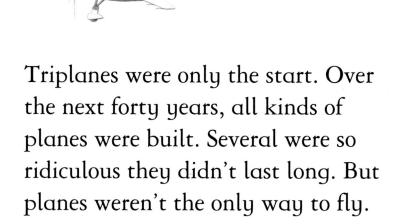

Triplanes were only the start. Over the next forty years, all kinds of planes were built. Several were so ridiculous they didn't last long. But planes weren't the only way to fly.

Like the first plane, the first hot-air balloon was invented by brothers. The Montgolfiers, who were French, noticed that hot air rises. They had the idea of trapping it in a big bag, which would then float up.

They filled their first balloon by holding it over a fire. Their second balloon even had passengers: a duck, a rooster and one very scared sheep.

Soon, the Montgolfiers had built
a balloon large enough to carry
people. They put a fire in the base
to keep the air in the balloon hot.

Then, in 1804, a balloon-maker took the sea to the skies, building a balloon shaped like a giant fish. The captain kept it level by sliding a weight along a rope.

I've heard of flying fish but that's ridiculous.

The first balloon to cross the
Channel had wings. But they
didn't really work and it was
a much colder trip than
Louis Blériot's.

I'm f-f-
f-freezing.

The pilots worried they'd crash.
"We have to make the balloon
lighter!" shouted one in a panic,
and he took off all his clothes and
threw them into the sea.

In 1852, the Frenchman Henri Giffard tried something new. He built a balloon with a propeller, which was worked by a steam engine. It was so large, people called it an airship.

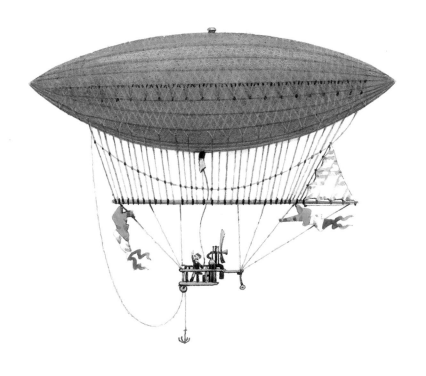

Fifty years later, airships had grown to the length of two blue whales. They looked a little like whales too. But, unlike whales, their insides were filled with huge gas tanks.

Dinner is served!

The most famous airship, the *Graf Zeppelin*, was a flying hotel.

In 1929, the *Graf Zeppelin* flew around the world in only three weeks. People were astounded. Nothing had gone around the world so fast. Then a mysterious fire destroyed an airship and no one wanted to fly them.

These gas bags look OK to me.

Besides, there was another invention that was much more fun.

Chapter 4

Helicopters

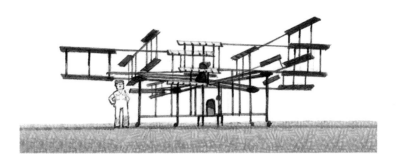

Flyers in France had combined a plane with a balloon. The result had an engine like a plane, but rotor blades rather than wings. So, it rose in the air like a balloon. They had invented...

...the helicopter!

In 1907, Paul Cornu made the world's first helicopter flight. But, as he was only in the air for 20 seconds and didn't even rise as high as a man, most people missed it.

Over 30 years went by before a helicopter flew properly. In 1939, Igor Sikorsky built his *VS-300* in America...

...and in 1940, he managed to fly it.

Igor's next helicopter, the *R4*, had space for two passengers. This so impressed the American Navy, they started to build *R4*s to use in the Second World War.

Helicopter designers went on to experiment with two rotor blades. These helped make the helicopter more stable. It could also lift more – like the *Chinook*, which can carry up to 44 passengers.

Today, helicopters aren't only used by armies and navies. They might be used to help the police keep an eye on traffic, or to rush a sick person to the nearest hospital.

Can't you go any faster?

They are even used to chase escaping criminals – and not only in movies.

One helicopter has been made to lift vast loads too heavy for trains or trucks. The "Skycrane" – which is half-copter, half-crane – can lift loads weighing as much as a house.

Chapter 5

Flying for fun

Just one hundred years after the Wright brothers' flight, planes, balloons and helicopters fill the sky.

42

Massive airports have been built
to cope with the hundreds of planes
which fly all over the world.

Thousands of passengers board planes every day, for work or travel. But many people also fly planes and gliders themselves for fun.

Gliders are light and very small inside. They also have no engine, which is the only thing they have in common with Sir George Cayley's machine.

It's a tight fit – but I love it!

To fly a glider, you must first be launched into the air.

The easiest way to do this is to get a tow from a friendly plane.

When the pilot is high enough, he'll release the tow rope and you'll be alone in the sky.

Gliders float on columns of warm air. After rising on one, pilots lower their gliders and race down to the next.

Pilots not only take maps, they take plenty of food and drink on a trip. If they find enough warm air to glide on, a flight can last all day.

Where did I put those sandwiches?

But gliding can be tricky. It's also expensive. So, many people go hang gliding instead.

The very first hang glider was invented by an American, Francis Rogallo, in the 1960s. His "Rogallo wing" is actually strapped to a flyer, who runs down a high hill to take off.

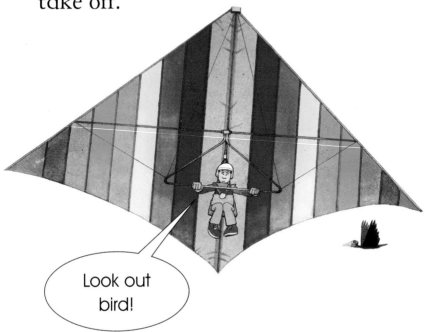

Look out bird!

Modern hang gliders
have thin nylon wings that
trap air underneath them to
fly. With a strong enough
wind, a flyer can stay up in
the air for hours.

49

Even if you don't like heights, you can still enjoy flying. Ever since Rheims, airshows have given plenty of opportunities for pilots to perform amazing stunts.

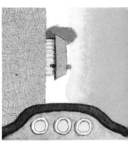

Some pilots roll their planes all
the way over. Inside the cockpit,
the pilot has a very strange view
of the earth.

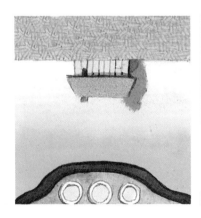

A popular trick that's almost as old as the Wright brothers' first plane is "wing-walking". It's also nearly as dangerous.

And I thought tightropes were high...

Flying low is dangerous too, but pilots sometimes fly low down to display their control skills.

The most experienced fliers can come so close to the ground their propellers cut through tape. A few even do this trick upside down.

Now that's just showing off...

Single planes can do all kinds of acrobatics in the sky. They fly in a big circle – "looping the loop" – or make the figure 8.

Clouds of white smoke trail behind them, to show people on the ground exactly where they've been.

Groups of planes
flying together can be
even more spectacular.
Led by one plane, the
others can fly in a line,
or make a "V" shape in
the sky, like a group of
flying ducks.

Chapter 6

Into space

I wonder how far this one will go...

Of course, planes, balloons and helicopters aren't the only way to fly. Thousands of years before any of them were invented, people in China were launching rockets.

56

But, as there are no written records, no one knows how well they flew.

Then, about two hundred years ago, armies began to use rockets in battle. By the time the Second World War broke out in 1939, rockets were more powerful.

Scientists realized they could use the power of rockets to reach space. On October 4, 1957, the first space machine was launched by the Russians. It was tiny and named *Sputnik 1*.

Just four years later, the Russians launched *Vostock 1*. Its pilot, Yuri Gagarin, became the first man to fly into space.

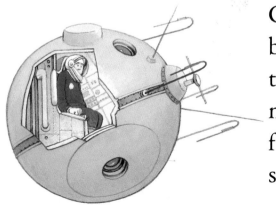

The Americans decided to join in. A race began to see who would be first to send a man to the Moon.

American scientists built *Saturn V*, the biggest rocket in the world. In July 1969, it blasted into space. Soon after that, Neil Armstrong became the first man to step onto the Moon's rocky surface.

Most of *Saturn V* was made up of booster engines. It needed vast amounts of power to blast itself into space. The astronauts were squashed into the tiny Command Module at the rocket's tip.

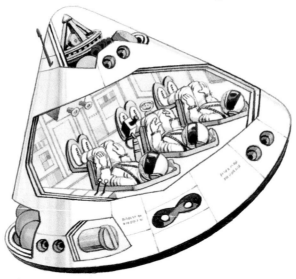

The booster engines fell away as the rocket flew higher. The Command Module was the only part to return to Earth.

Until 1980,
all space flights
were made with
rockets. But, as
they could only
be used once,
they weren't

very practical. So, American
scientists invented the space shuttle.

The shuttle is launched like a
rocket, but then the booster engine

and fuel tanks
drop off. The
shuttle's
engines take
over and it
flies... just like
a plane.

Today, shuttles carry astronauts and scientists into space to repair satellites and carry out experiments. People often live and work on them for months at a time.

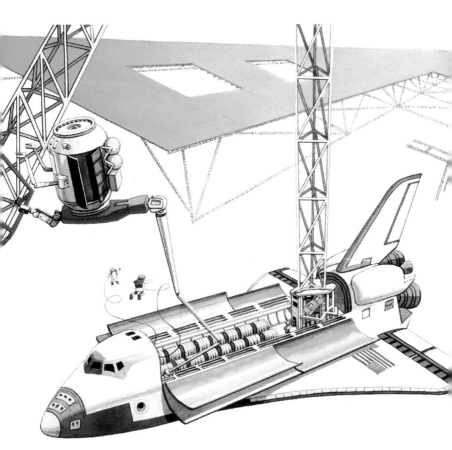

Shuttles have also been used
to put giant telescopes in space.

As you read this, astronomers
are learning more about parts
of the universe millions of miles
away...

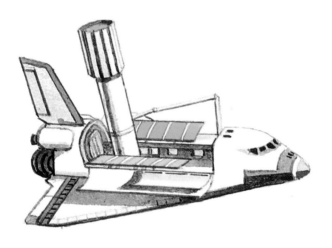

...places that people may even fly
to one day.

Based on original material by Christopher Rawson
Original consultant: Bill Gunston

Designed by
Katarina Dragoslavić

This edition first published in 2007 by Usborne Publishing Ltd.,
Usborne House, 83-85 Saffron Hill, London EC1N 8RT, England.
www.usborne.com
Copyright © 2007, 2004, 1981 Usborne Publishing Ltd.

64